A Dandelion addresses the sensitive issue of "Flowerism."

A Dandelion

ANDREW EVERSTINE

iUniverse books may be ordered through booksellers or by contacting:

iUniverse
1663 Liberty Drive
Bloomington, IN 47403
www.iuniverse.com
844-349-9409

Because of the dynamic nature of the Internet, any web addresses or links contained in this book may have changed since publication and may no longer be valid. The views expressed in this work are solely those of the author and do not necessarily reflect the views of the publisher, and the publisher hereby disclaims any responsibility for them.

Any people depicted in stock imagery provided by Getty Images are models, and such images are being used for illustrative purposes only. Certain stock imagery © Getty Images.

ISBN: 978-1-6632-4049-1 (sc)
ISBN: 978-1-6632-4051-4 (hc)
ISBN: 978-1-6632-4050-7 (e)

Library of Congress Control Number: 2022910198

Print information available on the last page.

iUniverse rev. date: 06/06/2022

This Book is dedicated to

Ashli C. Everstine, M.D.

Special Thanks to

My wife, Woyeni, for supporting me with this journey.

Our daughter...Julia Gonsalves, for editing
this book. Your input was priceless!

"Cheers Dears!!!"

Once, there lived a Dandelion named Sally. She looked just like the other Dandelions, but she was full of hope and determination. This gave her a positive outlook on life, even though Dandelions were sometimes treated poorly.

A party was to take place. An invitation list was planned to be posted at the Town Hall.

The day finally arrived. A large crowd was outside...ready to see the list.

The doors opened and the flowers rushed through. They hurried down the hall and into the Courtyard.

Sally, bless her heart, patiently walked in after everybody.

Some flowers were so excited to see their names on the list that they almost lost a bud or two by jumping up and down. Others weren't so cheery. Some of the ones that didn't get invited didn't seem to care. Others bowed their heads.

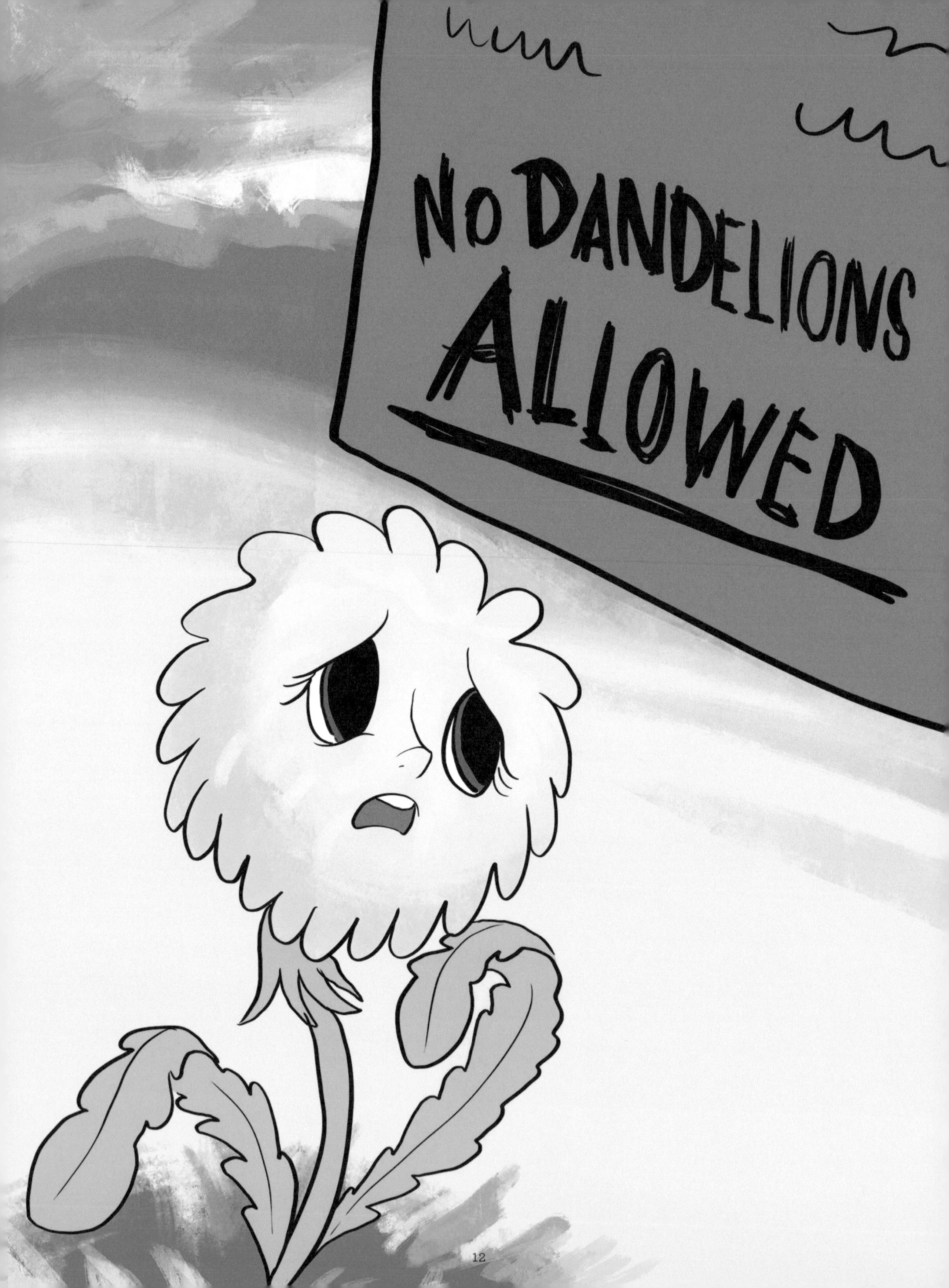
NO DANDELIONS
ALLOWED

She made her way up to the front. Sadly, the name Sally Budfield was not on it.

Something caught her eye.

There was a note on the bottom that read, "No Dandelions Allowed!"

Sally was crushed. She tried to hold back the tears. Her mother always told her to remain strong because sad tears made her colors fade.

14

When the day of the party arrived, Sally found peace.

Sally showed true character by saying, "I hope you have a great time!"

Some flowers said, "Thanks so much!"

Others didn't say a word because Sally was a Dandelion and Dandelions were simply not invited.

Suddenly, she remembered that her aunt had given her some special pink powder for her birthday.

On that day, her Aunt said, "You can only use this once and you will **_know_** when to use it."

Sally didn't understand at the time, but now it was clear.

She raced into her clump of grass and into her room. There it was, waiting patiently.

"If I put this pink powder on my head, it will disguise my yellow, and no one will have a clue that I am a Dandelion.

She looked at the powder, then at herself in the mirror. She added more and more pink powder until her head was totally pink. With one last look in the mirror, she left for the party, even though she still wasn't invited.

Sally had an idea. It seemed easy enough. She would enter through the kitchen and say she must have gotten lost.

Her plan worked and before she knew it, she had a mug of hot chocolate in her hand and was mingling with the other flowers. She had to play it smart because she still was, and would always be, a Dandelion.

"My, my," said Rose, "I don't believe I've seen your kind around here."

"I'm from up north," Sally quickly replied, smiling, and added, "I'm a Yankee Carnation."

"'Don't suppose I've heard of that one before," another flower replied.

"We're a rare flower," said Sally. "I'm sure," said Rose, and they all moved on.

Sally had passed the first test. She gracefully walked over to the buffet table, to see what they had to eat. She was surprised to see her favorite food...Fried Cajon Bees...on the buffet table.

She put some onto her plate. She loved spicy foods. Sally's Dad said that it was the stinger that made them spicy...a spice that humans could not tolerate.

She walked around, humming a familiar tune.

"Are you humming Twinkle, Twinkle Little Star?" Lilac asked.

"Yes, I was," Sally said.

"I love that that song!" Lilac said.

"What are you doing talking to **_her?!_**" Lily asked.

Lilac didn't answer but apologized to Sally and walked away.

"What kind of flower did you say you were?" Lily asked.

"I'm a Y-Y-Yankee Carnation," Sally hesitantly replied.

"You look familiar. I can't put my bud on it, but something about you...." Lily said.

"Yes, she does look rather familiar," Magnolia said, then added, "Are you a distant relative of the Dandelion? Because that would mean that you really shouldn't be here."

Sally was frightened and didn't say a word.

"Can you **_imagine?!_** A relative of the Dandelion at *this* party?!!" Lily said.

Suddenly, there was a fire on the stove. Flowers threw water on the grease fire, which only added to the flames. Fire quickly spread everywhere!!!

Sally, always quick on her buds, yelled, "Somebody dial 911 for help!!!"

She helped Rose to safety, even though she was rude to her.

Flowers pushed each other out of the way to get out of the
burning building.

Within a short time, the fire department showed up and
quickly went to work.

Many of the Volunteers were Dandelions!

Sally kept going back inside to save more flowers.

What Sally didn't realize was that each time she went back inside, some of the pink would wear off from the smoke and heat. By the time she made six or seven trips, she was a Yellow Dandelion again.

The Volunteer Dandelions helped rescue flowers as well.

Within a short time, the fire was out and everyone was rescued.

"Hey!!!" a flower yelled, "She's a Dandelion!!!"

The crowd became silent.

"Dandelion or no Dandelion... She did what many of us chose not to do!" Lily said then added, "She and the Volunteer Dandelions saved others, while many of us were busy saving ourselves!!!"

Rose stood up and said, "We are going to have a party and *ALL* the Dandelions will be invited. Sally, I never knew that Dandelions had so much character, courage and grace. I apologize for that."

"Me too," a voice from the crowd said.

"Me too," ... "Me too," other flowers said.

"Us too," many others added.

"Thank you very much. I am sure that many of us Dandelions would *LOVE* to go," Sally said, letting the joyful tears flow. Her mom also had said that happy tears made her colors brighter.

They held a party and *everyone* was invited. Those who still thought they were better than Dandelions did not attend.

The Party was outside. It wasn't as nice as the previous party, but Dandelions knew how to have fun.

The Dandelions made everyone feel welcome and by the end of the party, lifelong friendships had begun.

And everyone lived *humbly* ever after.

The Beginning

Printed in the United States
by Baker & Taylor Publisher Services